What's the Worst That Can Happen?

PRAISE FOR *STORYSHARES*

"One of the brightest innovators and game-changers in the education industry."
– Forbes

"Your success in applying research-validated practices to promote literacy serves as a valuable model for other organizations seeking to create evidence-based literacy programs."

- Library of Congress

"We need powerful social and educational innovation, and Storyshares is breaking new ground. The organization addresses critical problems facing our students and teachers. I am excited about the strategies it brings to the collective work of making sure every student has an equal chance in life."
– Teach For America

"Around the world, this is one of the up-and-coming trailblazers changing the landscape of literacy and education."
- International Literacy Association

"It's the perfect idea. There's really nothing like this. I mean wow, this will be a wonderful experience for young people."   - Andrea Davis Pinkney, Executive Director, Scholastic

"Reading for meaning opens opportunities for a lifetime of learning. Providing emerging readers with engaging texts that are designed to offer both challenges and support for each individual will improve their lives for years to come. Storyshares is a wonderful start."
- David Rose, Co-founder of CAST & UDL

What's the Worst That Can Happen?

Robert Wonders

STORYSHARES

Story Share, Inc.
New York. Boston. Philadelphia

Published in the United States by Story Share, Inc.

Storyshares
Story Share, Inc.
24 N. Bryn Mawr Avenue #340
Bryn Mawr, PA 19010-3304
www.storyshares.org

Inspiring reading with a new kind of book.

Interest Level: Middle School
Grade Level Equivalent: 3.4

9781642615739

Book design by Storyshares

Printed in the United States of America

Storyshares Presents

1

"There are only 10 seconds left in this Middle School championship soccer game. We have a tie between the Waterford Warriors and the Eastside Eagles. There are many injuries in this hard-fought game. Waterford has only one player left on the field: goalie Tyler Jackson.

"Here come the Eagles! Diaz passes the ball to Arnez on the left. Jackson moves to cover that side. A pass back over to Martin. He boots a bullet straight at the goal.

"AMAZING! Jackson somersaults in mid-air and blocks the shot. The ball falls to the ground. Jackson takes control of the ball and leaves the goal. He kicks it straight at Eastside's Smith. Jackson moves around him. Smith falls. Still sprinting forward, Jackson drives between two Eastside players...

"Only two seconds left. The remaining Eastside players surround the goal. There's no way Jackson can score... but wait! Jackson kicks the soccer ball up over his head. He leaps up, twists in midair, and kicks the ball again. Look at that ball spin!

"The ball is curving around all the Eastside players. Eastside goalie Murphy leaps for it. He catches it, but Jackson's shot was so powerful it sends Murphy and the ball into the goal. The horn sounds.

"Jackson did it! He scored. The crowd goes wild! Waterford's student representative, Lily Franklin, looks ecstatic. She is about to present the Most Valuable Player trophy to Jackson..."

"We're all waiting, Mr. Jackson," repeated Mr. Scales.

"Seven," whispered Greg Keaty from behind Tyler.

"Seven," repeated Tyler, with no idea what it meant.

"Seven is correct. Thank you, *Mr. Keaty,*" said Mr. Scales. His reply was far too slow to be kind. "Mr. Keaty, Mr. Jackson. Two extra Algebra chapters, due tomorrow."

"I should have whispered softer," said Greg, once he and Tyler were walking down the Waterford Middle School hallway to their sixth-grade study hall.

"I shouldn't have been daydreaming," mumbled Tyler.

Greg was Tyler's best friend. He knew Tyler was distracted by something. Greg followed Tyler's gaze. Of course it ended at Lily Franklin. She was standing down the hall talking to a group of her friends.

"Sure you're not daydreaming now?"

Tyler's face turned every shade of red. Then he sighed.

"You should go talk to her," said Greg. "I hear she's nice. She won't bite."

"She's always with a group of friends. Besides…"

"Besides what?"

"I'm just not that impressive. Lots of guys are smarter, better looking, better athletes..."

"Well, you gotta try. What's the worst that can happen?"

They ambled down to study hall, their last period of the day. Tyler sat in his chair and looked past his homework. His imagination started to take over once more...

What's the worst that can happen? Tyler asks himself as he drops back to pass the ball. He's still in the game, despite the cast wrapped around his broken foot.

There are only thirty seconds left. Waterford is down by four points to the Millbridge Mustangs. This could be the last play of the game. The entire Waterford home crowd holds its breath as Jackson runs with the ball. He glances into the stands. Even Lily Franklin has turned away, too afraid to watch.

None of Tyler's receivers are open. He ignores his broken foot and runs toward the sidelines. His usual blazing speed is hampered by his cast, but his natural athleticism allows him to avoid each would-be tackler. He's just two feet from the goal line. Jackson musters all his strength and dives over the Millbridge defenders. He seems to hang in the air...

"The bus won't wait forever, Mr. Jackson," said Mrs. Klitz, who supervised the study hall session. "Study hall is over. Most students can't wait for the final bell. Are you spending the night here?"

Tyler said nothing as he gathered his books and rushed out to his waiting bus. At the back of the school grounds, he saw Lily Franklin. She was walking with Samara Noorani toward the neighborhood behind the school.

So, she lives in walking distance of Waterford...

2

On the bus ride home, Tyler tried to come up with a plan to impress Lily. His schoolwork was only average. He wasn't a sports star. He'd have to think some more before he talked to her.

Tyler's mother met him as he got off the bus in front of his house. "Remember, you promised to mow the lawn after school today," said his mom. "It won't take you very long. I need to run down to the market to get a few things. I'll be back shortly."

Tyler sighed and went inside his house to change his clothes. Then he walked to the garage and pulled out the old push mower.

He started it up and began mowing the front yard. *How boring!* thought Tyler. *Oh well, just one foot after the other...*

"What endurance! Each foot is just flying after the other. This boy was born to run. Jane, how often do you see a boy this age sprint a marathon?"

"Well, John, he doesn't hold the marathon world record for nothing. Here we are today at the Boston Marathon. Tyler Jackson is already a half mile ahead of his nearest competitor."

"Look at that, Jane! He doesn't even slow down to grab water!"

"And that hill, John. I think he's running faster going up it! He truly is a finely-tuned running machine...

"What are you doing with that machine?" yelled his dad.

Mr. Jackson had just come home from work to find a winding path cut randomly across the lawn.

Tyler stopped and looked around him. *Oops*, he thought. *Guess I wasn't paying attention.*

There wasn't a straight line to be found. There were areas of lawn that had never even met the mower's blades.

"Should I start over?" asked Tyler sheepishly.

His dad sighed. "We'll be eating dinner soon. Most of the lawn is mowed. Maybe we'll fix it after we eat. Go inside and wash up."

3

Today was the day. Today he would do it. Her friends would just have to wait.

Should I introduce myself? Should I ask her out on a date? Too fast! Maybe I can walk her home? Still too fast. I could suggest that we sit together at lunch?

Whoa! There she is. With three of her friends. Why is my heart pounding so hard? Breathe. I'll just walk over, excuse myself, and ask to speak to her briefly...

Suddenly, Tyler's books flew out of his arms. They went scattering all over the hall floor. Gil Stanton walked past him without acknowledging that he had knocked into Tyler from behind. He kept walking... right toward Lily!

What?

Tyler ignored his books on the floor and stared in horror as Gil began speaking to her.

He's speaking to her. She's answering him. I thought Gil was seeing Holly Cunningham. They're walking together, alone, down the hall...

"Relax, Tyler," said Greg, as he walked over from his locker. He bent over and helped Tyler collect his books. "I saw the whole thing. They're on the student council committee together. Gil's too much of a jerk for Lily to be interested in him."

"Thanks," said Tyler, as Greg handed him his last book. "Did she smile at him? Because if she did, that means..."

"Will you relax? Yes, she smiled at him. She smiles at everyone. I told you, she's a nice person. That doesn't mean they're getting married."

Tyler closed his eyes and took a deep breath. He needed a plan, an excellent plan, to break the ice with Lily.

4

Tyler stood on the Waterford Middle School gym floor listening to Coach Panelli explain the rules for the intramural boys' basketball tournament.

Tournament is a loose term, thought Tyler.

The tournament was held after school over two days that week. There were only four
teams, with eight people on a team. That was a lot considering Waterford wasn't a large school. But only four people on a team played at a time.

Tyler wasn't a bad player. He just wasn't very good. Since his parents wanted him to do something athletic, he participated in the tournament.

He looked around the gym and his heart seemed to stop. Lily Franklin was over at the gymnastics bars. Mr. Panelli's instructions faded from his mind.

What is it about her? Her smile? Maybe. She is smart and kind — I think. But so are other girls.

He couldn't stop thinking about her, at least when he wasn't daydreaming about winning Olympic gold medals or raising a shiny championship cup above his head in front of adoring fans.

"Okay then," said Coach Panelli. "First game starts tomorrow, right here after school."

Tyler had a thought. *Maybe if Lily is here after school, she'll watch the games. Maybe, if I don't embarrass myself, I can impress her. Or at least show her that I exist.*

Tyler decided he should practice before the late bus left. He took a basketball from the ball bin and walked outside where the courts offered more privacy. Tyler stood at the foul line and eyed the rim.

"Another great crossover dribble by Jackson. Our guest student of the month, Lily Franklin, smiles her approval from her guest seat on the Waterford bench. Blake Madden of the Standish Middle School Steers slips to the floor as he tries in vain to cover Jackson. Jackson has a free shot at midcourt. Nothing but net! We have a tie score! Lily Franklin stands and applauds!

"The Standish Middle School Steers bring the ball down with 13 seconds on the clock. Manetti passes to Krafton. Stolen by Jackson! He throws it toward the Waterford Middle School rim. He races ahead of everyone to follow his throw. Jackson leaps from the top of the foul line, up over the rim, catches the rebound — a pass to himself — and slams it home just as the buzzer..."

"You gonna shoot that or just stand there?" Gil Stanton grinned and tossed up a perfect outside shot. Nothing but net.

Well, he's an eighth-grader, thought Tyler. *I still have time to get that good.*

Gil, still grinning, looked at Tyler and shook his head.

Good, thought Tyler. *Gil is leaving with his friends. Now I can concentrate.*

Tyler walked close to the rim, put up a point-blank shot, and missed.

5

"I think we might actually win," said Greg.

He sat next to Tyler on the bench. They watched their group, Group A, beat Group D in the first game of the two-day tournament.

"Looks like we'll play the winner, either Group B or Group C, for the championship tomorrow," said Tyler. "Too bad I was only in this game for five minutes. At least I managed not to embarrass myself."

"I was in less than that." Greg grinned. "Guess they wanted to keep the score down."

Tyler wouldn't have minded being in the game, but sitting on the bench allowed him to watch Lily from across the gym. She was on a large dance mat, twirling a ribbon in a dance routine. She wasn't very good. She kept getting tangled in the ribbon as it trailed behind her. But she just smiled that smile of hers and kept going.

Tyler admired her attitude. She was trying, but wasn't taking it too seriously. Not like Jessica Herd, who had stormed off in a rage earlier. Tasha Billings had started before Jessica finished her routine and had accidentally stepped on her ribbon.

"Earth to Tyler," said Greg. "Must be a Lily alert." Greg followed Tyler's gaze. "And there she is..."

The final horn interrupted Greg. Tyler and Greg stood up and joined their teammates as they all walked off the court and into the locker room.

We won, thought Tyler. *Okay, now on to the championship game. Lily* did *look over at our game a few times, but she never came over. At least she's here. Maybe tomorrow she'll watch the championship game.*

6

Lily's here. Watching in the stands. But I haven't even been in the game yet.

"If we win, are you and I still champions? Even if we didn't get to play?" asked Greg. He and Tyler had sat on the bench for the whole game so far.

"What? No." Tyler refocused his attention on the game. "It only matters if we get in the game and make it to the end. We're only ahead by a point, and there are 30 seconds left. Guess I shouldn't have been late to Coach Panelli's gym class so often."

"It might help if Coach P actually thought you and I could win the game," said Greg.

The horn sounded for a timeout. Tyler's group still led Group C by one point.

"Okay, everyone. It's our ball. Just protect it for 30 seconds," said Coach Panelli. "We have a one-point lead. Who hasn't played yet?" Tyler, Greg, and Cyril Padaway all raised their hands.

"Okay, you people are in for Jim, Alex, and Stan. Just don't be heroes and the game will be ours."

Yes! thought Tyler.

He had a plan, and it *did* involve being a hero. All he needed was to hold the ball when the game ended. He didn't have to shoot or score. If they won, his teammates would be so happy that he'd get credit just by association. His teammates would probably carry him off the court on their shoulders in triumph. Lily would be enthralled. But first he had to get the ball and hold it. Otherwise he'd just be invisible and in the background.

Tyler waved his arms madly for the ball. Mark Demeter threw the ball to Cyril Padaway. Cyril dribbled for a few seconds before passing it back to Mark.

20 seconds left on the clock. Mark looked around, then passed the ball to Greg. Tyler saw his chance. He stepped in front of Greg and grabbed the ball.

15 seconds left. He didn't even have to pass the ball. He just had to dribble for a few seconds and then hold it until the game ended. Then his team would win. He'd be the hero. His teammates would carry him on their shoulders to the locker room. Lily would have to notice him...

Suddenly, from nowhere, a hand came down on the ball. Jimmy Gaston from the C team swiped the ball cleanly and knocked it to the floor.

Tyler dove for the ball. Instead of grabbing it back, he fell face down onto the court. As he fell, he knocked the ball toward the other end, where Conner Erio was waiting to grab it.

10 seconds left. Conner Erio had never taken a shot in his life. Connor Erio had never touched a basketball ball in his life. And yet Conner picked up the ball and turned toward the basket...

5 seconds. Conner closed his eyes. Conner threw the ball.

3 seconds. The ball went in.

The buzzer sounded.

Conner Erio on the C team had just single-handedly beaten Tyler and the A team. Well, not single-handedly. Tyler was the one who got Conner the ball.

Tyler was still on the floor. Everything seemed to move in slow motion. Coach Panelli was screaming at him. He turned his head toward Lily. She was cringing like the rest of the people in the stands. His teammates were waving their arms in disbelief, also screaming at Tyler. He heard none of it.

What's the worst that can happen?

For reasons he didn't quite understand, he sat up on the court and started laughing. He laughed at his own foolishness. He laughed at his silly plan. Even if it had worked, Lily probably would still not know he existed.

People all around stared at him like he had lost his mind. Team C triumphantly marched off to the locker room to celebrate. Conner Erio was on their shoulders.

Tyler had blown it with Lily. She probably thought, along with everyone else at school, that he was the world's biggest idiot.

What's the worst that can happen? Probably this, thought Tyler.

Still sitting on the court alone and laughing, he glanced at Lily again. She was walking down from the stands, listening to her friends as they shook their heads and laughed. His own laughter faded to a smile.

Time to get up and face the music.

He slowly walked into the boys' locker room. There were so many shouts from his teammates that they all blended together into one muddled scream.

Tyler ignored them all. *Lesson learned. I'm not an athlete. I will never will be a hero. I won't get the girl.*

That stung.

I should at least approach Lily. I could apologize for being dumb? Try to make light of it all? Tell her how I feel about her? Ask her if she even knows who I am?

Arg!

7

Tyler quickly showered and changed, then walked out of the locker room and into the school hallway alone. Most of his teammates had already left. No one wanted anything to do with him, anyway.

He felt numb. Not good or bad, just numb. With his head down, he slowly walked down the hall toward the exit. He looked up and thought that his eyes were playing tricks on him. It certainly looked like Lily was standing alone against the wall.

Great. One last humiliation before the day is out.

"Excuse me," Lily said. She turned and walked up to him. "You're Tyler, right?"

Tyler, standing with his mouth slightly open, just nodded.

"I hope I'm not bothering you..."

He silently shook his head "no."

"...But I hope you're all right. At first, I was worried that you had hurt yourself. I was confused when I saw you laughing, but then I realized that laughing like that took a lot of courage." Lily smiled at him.

"I mean, you looked pretty bad..." She suddenly looked horrified. "I don't mean that you *look* bad, it's just that you were sprawled out on the floor, and your team lost... But you took it with grace and humor."

Tyler suddenly wasn't numb anymore. Did an impossible ray of hope just break through the bleak clouds?

"I did look bad," he said with a sheepish grin. "You thought I had courage?"

"I think any of the other boys would have cried or screamed or pouted," said Lily. "I like that you laughed. Sorry, I'm probably bothering you. I should go home now."

"Wait," Tyler said quickly. "I mean, wait — *please*. Trust me, you're not bothering me. You just said the nicest thing that anyone has ever said to me. Thank you for the compliment. How did you know my name?"

Lily's face reddened. "I asked Tracy."

"Oh," said Tyler. He didn't even know who Tracy was. "Well, I guess I'll take the *late* late bus today. It gets dark early. Do you always walk home?"

"Who told you I walked home?"

It was Tyler's turn to turn red. He scrunched up his face. "I noticed you walking home a few times. Do you live in the neighborhood?"

Lily smiled, pleased that Tyler had noticed her. "Yes, over on Milford street. When I walk home, though, it's usually earlier and a lot lighter out."

"Well, I can walk with you and see you safely to your door. I mean... if you want..."

Lily giggled softly. "That would be nice. But how will you get home?"

"Hmm, good point. Well, I can walk home from your house."

Lily smiled again. "I'm sure my mom will drive you home. She should be home from work by then."

They talked all the way to Lily's house. On the way, Tyler didn't kick one soccer goal, throw one touchdown pass, win one race, or sink one basket.

About The Author

Bob Wonders is a designer who lives with his wife and son in Manlius, NY. He discovered Story Shares when looking for reading material to help increase his son's interest in reading. He applauds Story Shares's efforts in helping teens and young adults improve their literacy.

About The Publisher

Story Shares is a nonprofit focused on supporting the millions of teens and adults who struggle with reading by creating a new shelf in the library specifically for them. The ever-growing collection features content that is compelling and culturally relevant for teens and adults, yet still readable at a range of lower reading levels.

Story Shares generates content by engaging deeply with writers, bringing together a community to create this new kind of book. With more intriguing and approachable stories to choose from, the teens and adults who have fallen behind are improving their skills and beginning to discover the joy of reading. For more information, visit storyshares.org.

Easy to Read. Hard to Put Down.

What's the Worst That Can Happen?

www.ingramcontent.com/pod-product-compliance
Lightning Source LLC
Chambersburg PA
CBHW071229170626
46809CB00005BA/1992